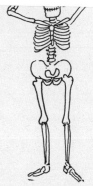

All About My Skeleton

ACTIVITY BOOK

by Sonia W. Black

Illustrations by Cristina Ong

SCHOLASTIC INC.

New York Toronto London Auckland Sydney

ISBN 0-590-48721-3

12 11   9/9

Printed in the U.S.A.   14

First Scholastic printing, August 1994

You can check your answers to the puzzles in this book on pages 31 and 32.

A Whole Lot of Bones!

Here's a real eye-opener—the human body has 206 bones! They make up your skeleton.

The skeleton bones at the bottom of this page are shown in the picture below. Find them and circle them.

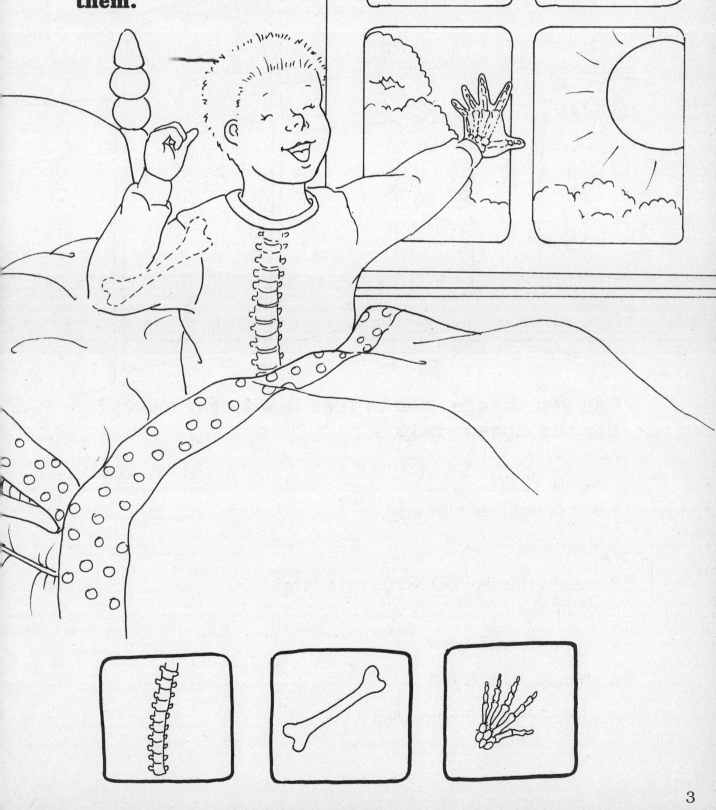

Here a Bone, There a Bone . . .

Everywhere a bone. . . . The bones in your skeleton come in all shapes and sizes. From your head down to your toes, there are big ones, small ones, round ones, flat ones. . . . Altogether they give your body its very own shape.

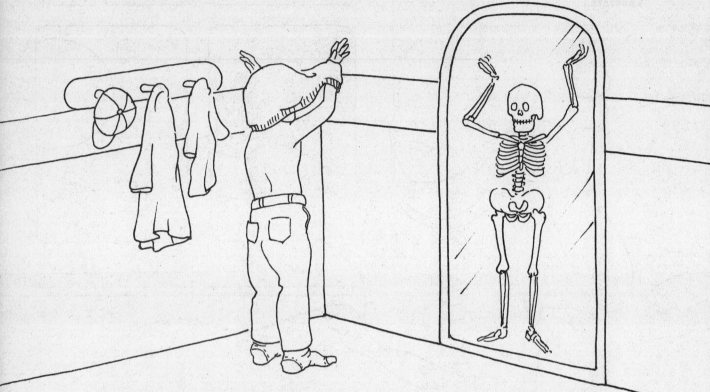

Can you change HEAD to TOES in six easy moves? Use the clues to help.

	H E A D
1. the opposite of alive	__ __ __ __
2. a good act	__ __ __ __
3. sign at the zoo: DO NOT _____ THE ANIMALS!	__ __ __ __
4. you walk with these	__ __ __ __
5. rhymes with "bees"	__ __ __ __
6. another word for enemies	__ __ __ __
	T O E S

No Spare Parts!

This shape-ly word search is also filled with bones. Actually, there are body parts and bones. Look down, across, backwards, and diagonally. Circle each word as you find it. Look for: FINGERS, TOES, ANKLE, KNEE, NECK, HAND, WRIST, ELBOW, ARM, HIP, THIGH, LEG, FOOT, JAW, CHEST, HEAD, and SHOULDERS— and eleven BONES.

```
              O N E
            S E N O B
          K S O P B O B
          O C I B W O O
          H E A D B
            J N O
            O K B
    S S H O U L D E R S S
    R   S T S E H C E   O
    E   B E S H A N D   W
    G   O L R O O       R
    N   B M B B B       I
    I   O F O O T       S
    F   N N N S W       T
        S E G E L B B
        S S N S N O O
        B O N   N N N
        B T E   O S E
        O H S   B E S
        N I E   O N N
        E G N   N O O
        S H O   E B B
      T O E S B   S E E N K
```

The Hard and Soft of It

When you are first born, *all* your bones are rubbery soft. This soft, flexible bone is called *cartilage*. As you grow older, though, *most* of your bones become as hard as a rock.

Put an X on the people in the picture with the softest bones. Circle the person with the hardest bones.

Coded Cartilage

Only a few bones remain very, very soft, even when you are full grown.

The names of two body parts with soft cartilage are hidden in this coded puzzle. Use the code to find the names of these mystery parts.

S =    N =

R =   A =

E =   O =

___ ___ ___ ___

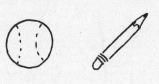

___ ___ ___ ___

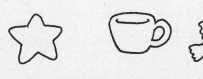

Long Live Bones!

Guess what? Your skeleton is alive! Yes, your bones are alive! That's why they grow longer and longer — and you get taller and taller. Of course, some people grow up to be a *lot* taller than others.

Study this basketball game very carefully. Try to remember *everything* that you see. Then take the quick memory quiz on the next page.

Time Out!

Circle the picture in each panel that's *exactly* the same as it appears on pages 8 and 9.

Foods to Grown On!

What's a good way to get strong, healthy, growing bones? Doctors say eating foods that have calcium is the answer.

Some of these foods are: MILK, YOGURT, ICE CREAM, CHEESE, EGGS, FISH, CHICKEN, and BROCCOLI. . . . Fill in their names in the crossword below. Some clue letters have already been filled in for you.

Head Protector!

Crash! Crunch! Ouch! Thank goodness for the strong, hard bone in your head. Like a crash helmet, it protects your brain from bumps, bruises, and dangerous injuries.

Color in the spaces with the letter "b" to see the name of that important bone.

The Whole Tooth!

Smile! Your skull also does the job of holding all 28 of your pearly white teeth. As you get older, four more teeth grow in and you end up with 32 altogether.

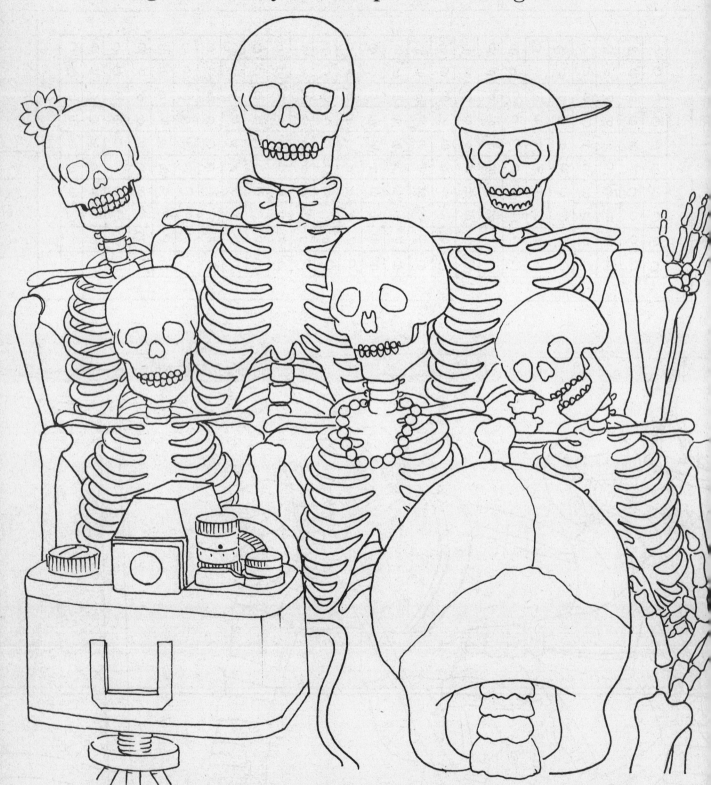

There are 8 things different in the picture on page 15. Find them and circle them.

On the Curve!

You've got 'em by the dozens! Your ribs, that is! Ribs are a set of bones that curve around your chest. There are twelve ribs on your right side and twelve on your left. They provide a safe covering for your heart, lungs, and stomach.

Color this scene any way you like.

We've Got Something in Common!

Scientists say there is an animal whose skeleton is a lot like yours.

Connect the dots from A to Z to see the mystery animal.

Look-alikes!

Check out these skeletons very carefully. Two of them are exactly alike. Can you figure out which ones they are?

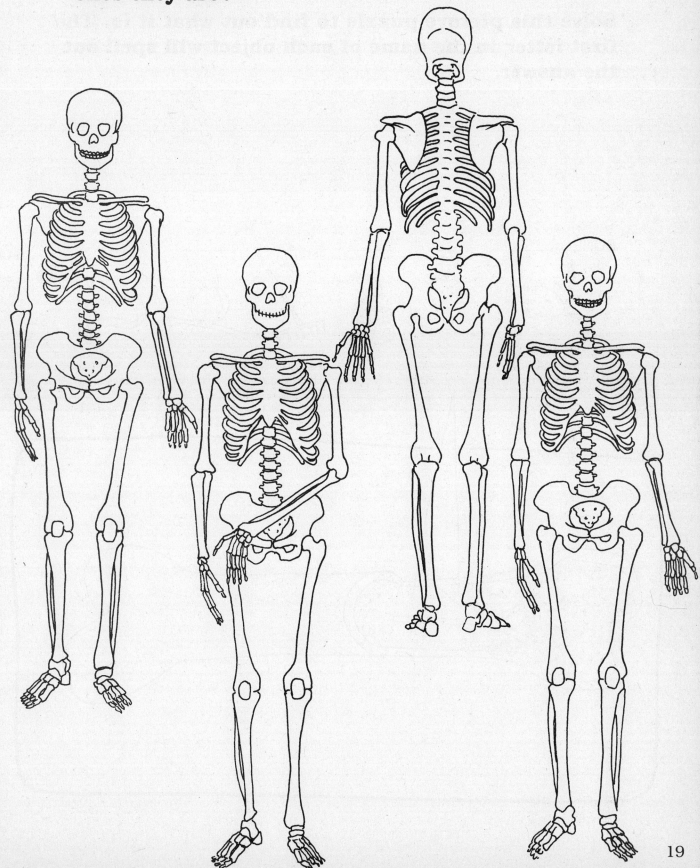

It's What's Inside That Counts!

Something squishy-soft is inside the center of some hard bones—like arm and leg bones. It's very important to your body because it helps to make your blood.

Solve this picture puzzle to find out what it is. The first letter in the name of each object will spell out the answer.

BONE ___ ___ ___ ___ ___ ___

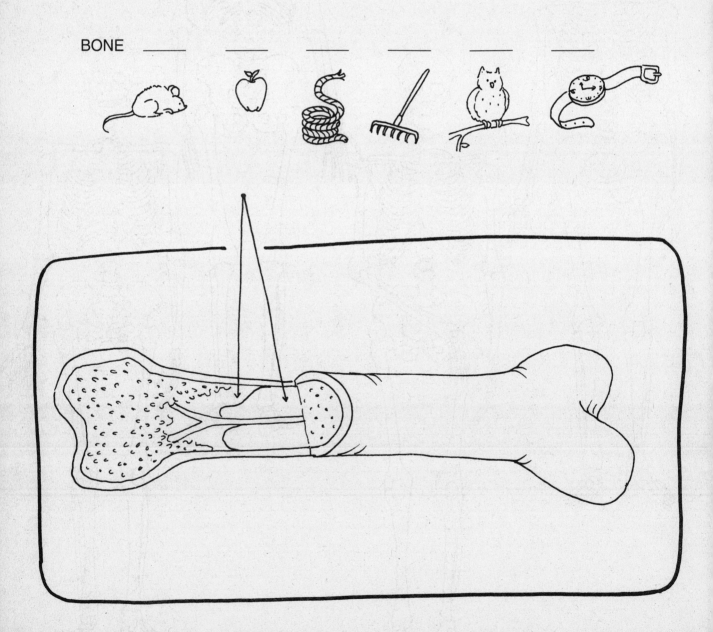

What's in a Word?

Actually, the part of the blood that squishy-soft something helps to make is your red blood cells. Red blood cells carry oxygen through your body.

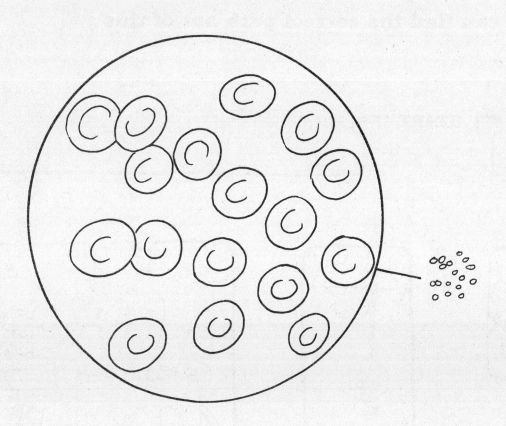

All the words in this puzzle have the letters R E D in them. Use the clues to help you fill in the missing letters in each word.

1. __ __ R E __ D   something you put through a needle.

2. R E __ D   what you do with a book.

3. __ R E __ D   you make sandwiches with this.

4. __ __ R E __ D   a kind of bed cover.

5. R E __ D __   _____, sct, go!

6. R E D __ __ __   to make something smaller.

It's A-maze-ing!

Would you believe you have 64 bones just in your hands and arms alone! Together, your feet have 58. And 34 bones run up and down your spine!

See if you can find the correct path out of this loony lab.

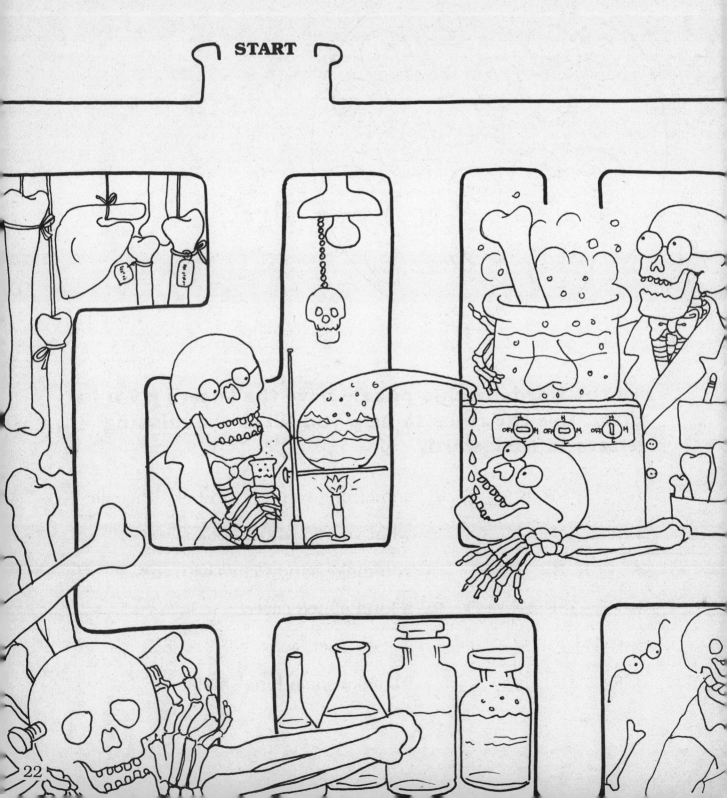

FINISH

The Connection!

Oh . . . the neck bone's connected to the shoulder bone. The shoulder bone's connected to the . . . The place where two bones are connected is called a *joint*.

Draw a line from column A to column B to match up the connecting joints.

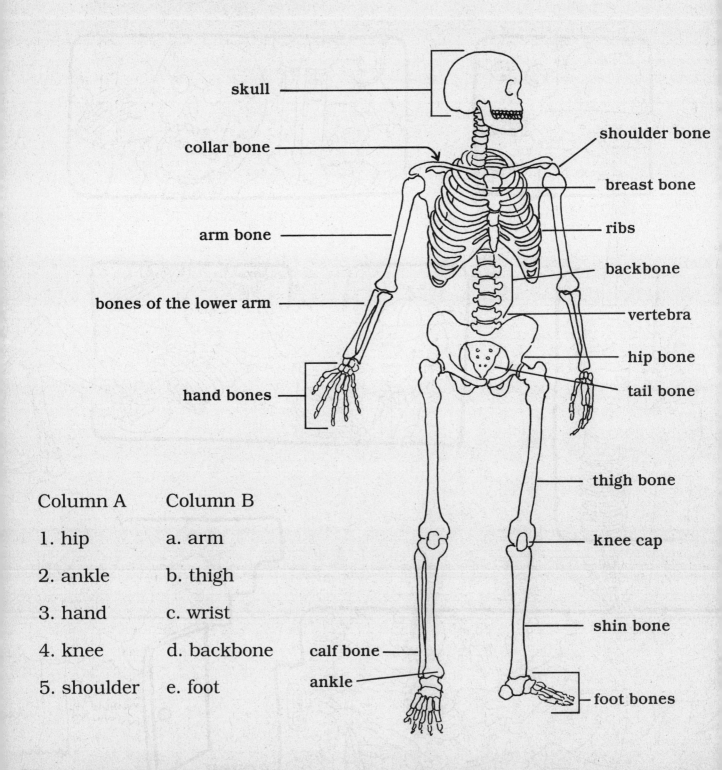

skull

collar bone

arm bone

bones of the lower arm

hand bones

shoulder bone

breast bone

ribs

backbone

vertebra

hip bone

tail bone

thigh bone

knee cap

shin bone

calf bone

ankle

foot bones

Column A	Column B
1. hip	a. arm
2. ankle	b. thigh
3. hand	c. wrist
4. knee	d. backbone
5. shoulder	e. foot

They've Got You Covered!

Your skeleton is covered with muscles and skin for protection. The muscles are attached to the bones at the joints.

These weight lifters have really big muscles. Put an X on the weight lifter who is bigger than the rest. Circle the one who is smaller.

No Strings Attached!

Simple puppets have only a few joints. But you have more than 200 joints in your skeleton. Why, there are over 50 joints in your hands alone!

Follow the tangled strings to find out which puppet belongs to whom.

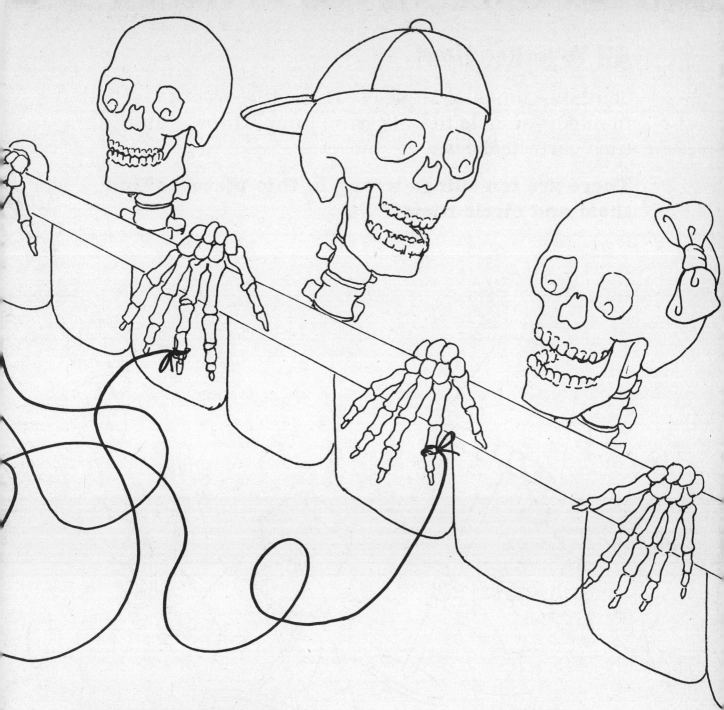

Hold Everything!

They're stretchy. They look like giant rubber bands. And they hold your joints together. What are they?

Cross out every X and O in the puzzle. The leftover letters spell out the answer.

XXLOXOOXIXGOXXAXXOOOMXOEXXONOXOTXXSOXO

— — — — — — — — — — —

All Together Now!

Joints! Ligaments! Muscles! These three work together to make you able to walk, run, jump, throw, catch, turn cartwheels, wave — move!

There are ten things wrong in this picture. Find them and circle them.

Bones at Rest!

Pssst! Just think . . . even as you sleep, your bones are growing. You'll be the ripe old age of, oh, about 20 years old before they stop growing. Nighty night. Zzzzzzzz . . .

Color this page any way you like.

Puzzle Answers

Page 3. A Whole Lot of Bones

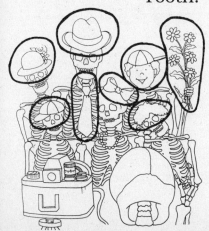

Page 4. Here a Bone, There a Bone . . .

HEAD, DEAD, DEED, FEED, FEET, FEES, FOES, TOES

Page 5. No Spare Parts!

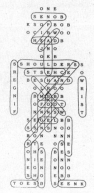

Page 6. The Hard and Soft of It

Page 7. Coded Cartilage

NOSE   EARS

Page 10. Time Out!

Page 11. Foods to Grow On!

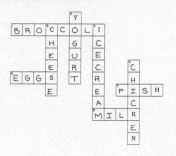

Pages 12 —13. Head Protector!

Pages 14 —15. The Whole Tooth!

Page 18. We've Got Something in Common!

Page 19. Look-alikes!

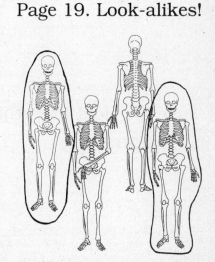

31

Page 20. It's What's Inside That Counts!

BONE MARROW

Pages 22 —23. It's A-maze-ing!

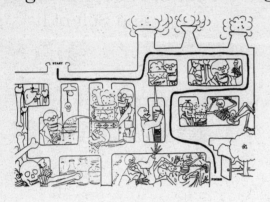

Page 25. They've Got You Covered!

Page 27. Hold Everything!

LIGAMENTS

Page 21. What's in a Word?

1. THREAD 2. READ 3. BREAD
4. SPREAD 5. READY 6. REDUCE

Page 24. The Connection!

Column A	Column B
1. hip	a. arm
2. ankle	b. thigh
3. hand	c. wrist
4. knee	d. backbone
5. shoulder	e. foot

Page 26. No Strings Attached!

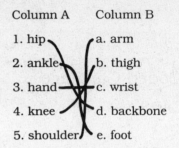

Pages 28 —29. All Together Now!